AND OTHER STORIES THAT STINK!

Scholastic Canada Ltd.

Toronto New York London Auckland Sydney
Mexico City New Delhi Hong Kong Buenos Aires

For all who have ever unleashed the wind within.   F. A.

557 Broadway, New York, NY 10012, USA

Scholastic Australia Pty Limited
PO Box 579, Gosford, NSW 2250, Australia

Scholastic New Zealand Limited
Private Bag 94407, Botany, Manukau 2163, New Zealand

Scholastic Children's Books
Euston House, 24 Eversholt Street, London NW1 1DB, UK

Library and Archives Canada Cataloguing in Publication

Arena Felice 1968-

Farticus Maximus and other stories that stink from Ancient Greece

.... 2011   j823'.92
C2011-902069-6

First published by Scholastic Australia in 2008.
This edition published in Canada by Scholastic Canada Ltd. in 2011.
Text and illustrations copyright © 2008 by Felice Arena.
All rights reserved.

6 5 4 3 2 1   Printed in Canada 121   11 12 13 14 15 16

AND OTHER STORIES THAT STINK!

WRITTEN & ILLUSTRATED BY
FELICE ARENA

Scholastic Canada Ltd.
Toronto New York London Auckland Sydney
Mexico City New Delhi Hong Kong Buenos Aires

CONTENTS

CHAPTERUS ONE

THE BEGINNING BUT NOT THE VERY BEGINNING, AKA THE FIERCEST GLADIATOR OF ALL TIME

If you're not a fan of blood and gore, stop reading now. If hard core bone-crushing battles to the death make you sick in the stomach, then seriously, don't read another line: this fable is not for you!

Go on! What are you waiting for? Skip to the next story . . .

Hmm? You're still here. Stubborn aren't you?

Oh, well, if you're going to continue to read this I'm going to have to swap some words, so that I don't totally freak you out.

So, the word "kill" will be replaced with "butterfly kiss" and "stab" will be replaced with "hug." Got it? That should take a little of the gruesomeness out of it. Yeah, yeah, I know that kind of sucks, but hey, I don't want to get into trouble with your folks and be the one responsible for you having nightmares tonight.

STAB = HUG

Who am I? That's not important, not for now, as this is not about me, but about one of the fiercest ancient Roman gladiators of all time: **Farticus Maximus!**

This story begins in the Colosseum in Rome, and our heroic warrior is about to get his head ripped off by a ferocious man-eating lion.

Packed in the greatest stadium in the world, the crowd has come to see one man only, the star attraction, Farticus Maximus.

And for a good hour or so, they haven't been disappointed. Farticus has single-handedly defeated eleven murderous criminals and four

The Colosseum....
that looks remarkably
like a cake!

MMMM! CAKE!

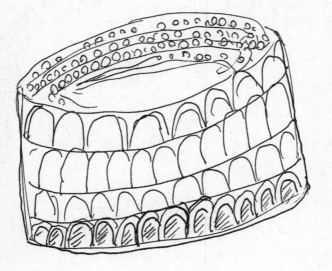

blood-hungry tigers: stunning them first with his
world-famous ... well, I'm getting ahead of myself.

As I said, a lion is about to bite Farticus's head
off. In an unexpected twist, the 150-kilogram big
cat has broken free from its chains and pounced

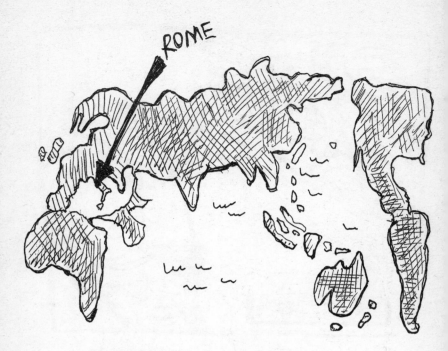

WORLD MAP - WONKY SCALE

on Farticus, pinning him to the ground. For the first time in his illustrious gladiator career, it looks like it's all over for our hero.

But let's freeze it there for now, and go back to the beginning ... yes, the very beginning ...

CHAPTERUS TWO

THAT'S MY BOY!

"There you go, Mrs Sandals," said the doctorus. "A healthy baby boy!"

Doctorus gently placed the baby in Helena Sandals's arms. By her bedside stood her loving husband, Petercus, and her first child, seven-year-old Juniper.

"So, what are you going to call him, Mommy?" asked Juniper, stepping in to take a closer look at his little brother.

"Your father and I have decided to call him Barticus," sighed Helena.

"PWHOH!" gasped Juniper. "I think Barticus just did his first **bigus poopus!** It stinks!"

Everyone agreed with young Juniper.

"By Janus! That's potent," coughed the doctorus. "I've never smelled anything like it in all my years as a doctorus!"

On closer inspection, Helena discovered that Barticus did not do a bigus poopus; not even a smallus poopus.

"You mean that was a **fart?**" she said, looking up at her husband, surprised.

"That's my boy," boasted Petercus proudly.

It was a known and true fact that the Roman emperor Claudius made it a law for all Romans to not hold their farts in, as this was an unhealthy thing to do. He encouraged everyone to let 'em rip **loud and proud**—especially at dinner banquets.

A few moments later, Barticus farted again. This time it was loud and deep—vibrating through the baby blanket. And again, the smell was as rotten as a sack of mule manure.

"He's *Farticus*, not Barticus!" declared Juniper, pinching his nose.

Everyone laughed, but little did they know that the farts of Barticus, who was from that time on always called Farticus, would make him a nuisance, but later also a hero to so many people . . .

CHAPTERUS THREE

GASSY PROBLEM

It wasn't long before the Sandals family realized that their second child was going to be more of a hardship for them than a joy. In the first year of his life, baby Farticus farted at least one hundred times a day—and all were vulgar and rotten. They were

HOW TO MAKE AN ORANGE-SCENTED SNOTUS RAG
BY MRS HELENA SANDALS

STEP I FIND SNOTUS RAG BIG ENOUGH TO TIE AROUND FACE.

MASSIVE DRIED SNOTUS STAIN

Dried crusty snotus stain

STEP II Soak snotus rag in bowl of orange juice. Leave in overnight.

orange juice

oranges

10

so rotten that the Sandals were forced to wear orange-scented snotus rags (handkerchiefs) around their noses to help combat part of the vile smell.

By the time Farticus was three, his farts had become unbearably ... well, unbearable. Friends and family stopped visiting; it was all too much for them to take. The thick stench

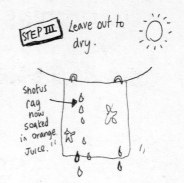

STEP III Leave out to dry.

Snotus rag now soaked in orange juice!!

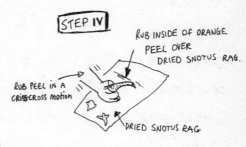

STEP IV

RUB INSIDE OF ORANGE PEEL OVER DRIED SNOTUS RAG.

RUB PEEL IN A CRISSCROSS motion

DRIED SNOTUS RAG

It smells like oranges!

STEP V

Tie snotus Rag around face. Make sure to cover your nose.

made many of them violently ill. And on windy
days the entire town would be affected by
Farticus's sickly, stinky odour wafting through the
streets.

"I'm sorry, Petercus," said Mr Sandals's best
friend, Graham, who was also the mayor of their
village. "You have to do something about your boy's
farting. We can't take it anymore!"

"There's nothing else we can do!" exclaimed
Farticus's dad. "We monitor what he eats and
drinks; we even made underpants out of iron! But

that didn't work 'cause his farts were so **fierce** that they melted away the metal."

Petercus shook his head in frustration. He paused and continued:

"We've also had five doctori check him out. They all concluded that there's nothing they can do since it is a physical thing. They think that Farticus's stomach intestines are twisted differently from everyone else's—and that's why his farts are so **putrid**. They did say when he's older he may be able to control his wind breaking."

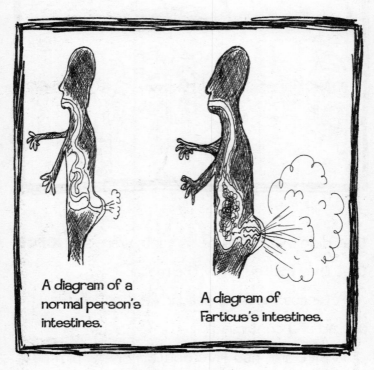

A diagram of a normal person's intestines.

A diagram of Farticus's intestines.

"I'm sorry," said Graham. "As the mayor of this town, I have to think of the villagers first. And we, the people, want you, no, *order* you and your family to **leave**."

Petercus had no choice—the Sandals would have to move. When Mr Sandals returned home to tell the bad news to his wife, he was shocked to discover his other son Juniper **unconscious** on the floor. Mrs Sandals was trying to revive him.

"Thank God you're here!" she panicked. "He was playing with Farticus!"

"What!?" choked Petercus, kneeling down beside Juniper. "What have we said about him getting too close to his brother!? Was he wearing his orange-scented snotus rag?"

"Yes, he was, but Farticus tripped and fell directly **bottomus first** on Juniper's face and farted! I told Farticus to wait outside!"

Mr Sandals gave Juniper mouth-to-mouth resuscitation and luckily he came to—coughing and spluttering.

"Enough's enough!" snapped Farticus's dad.

"What? What do you mean?" asked Mrs Sandals, as she helped Juniper back to his feet.

Petercus told his wife what Mayor Graham had said to him.

"But where are we going to go?"

"*We're* going nowhere!" said Petercus defiantly. "Farticus is always going to be a problem for us, Helena! We have to **get rid of him!**"

CHAPTERUS FOUR

OUT ON THEIR OWN

As it turned out there was no way Mrs Sandals
was going to get rid of her beloved son, even if his
smells did make her puke every day. So, in the end
she and Farticus left Petercus and Juniper and
went off to live on their own in an abandoned

WELCOME TO
NOWHERE
100 MILES TO ROME
20 MILES TO NEAREST VILLAGE
1 MILE TO DARK OMINOUS WOODS

ABANDONED HOUSE

farmhouse—in the middle of nowhere, close to no one.

For the next several years, life was extremely tough for Mrs Sandals and Farticus. They barely survived, living on eggs (they kept a couple of chickens a safe distance away from Farticus) and berries. Occasionally, passing Roman soldiers would give Mrs Sandals money and food in return for her delicious homemade chicken soup and her heavenly foot massages. Whenever this occurred, Farticus would hide away in some nearby woods, upwind of course.

When Farticus reached his teen years he was old enough to take long expeditions into dark forests and hunt. In fact, for the first time in Farticus's life his **farts came in handy**. He discovered he could use his gassy problem to his advantage. Whether he was hunting wild boars or majestic stags, he worked out that he could stun

them all with his farts. The smell would literally knock them unconscious for a minute or so, the same way he had bowled over his brother so many years before; and with a butterfly kiss here and butterfly kiss there, he'd end his prey's life, hugging them each time to the heart.

You may think it's cruel to butterfly kiss a wild animal, but for Farticus it was a matter of survival. It now meant that he and his mom wouldn't have to worry as much about where their next meal would come from—although it was never a sure thing, especially in winter, when most of the animals were hibernating.

When the hunting was scarce, Farticus did try to get some work. Once the perfect job had come up: working at a pigsty, or to be more specific, shovelling pig poopus. But this didn't work out as Farticus had hoped. The mixing of Farticus's farts and the stench from the pigs turned out to be a **mega-lethal gas**. Not only did it make the pigs pass out, it even knocked Farticus off his feet. He could always handle his own smells, but he got a dose of his own medicine

GAS CONTRIBUTION TO GLOBAL WARMING GRAPH

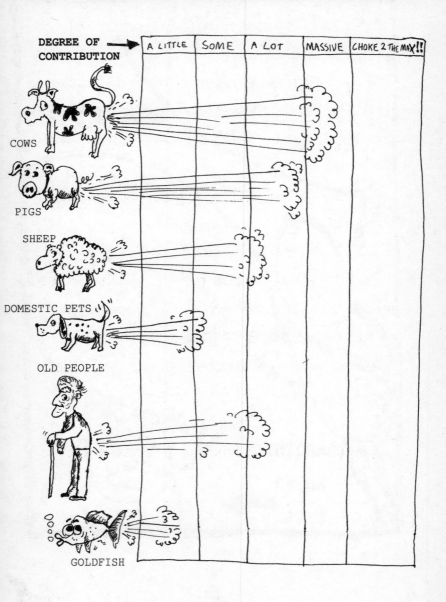

when faced with over a hundred farting pigs. He fainted and fell face first into pig poopus. Not surprisingly, he lost his job.

"Oh, Farticus, what are we going to do?" sighed his mother, as she rubbed more snotus rags with the rind of some oranges the Roman soldiers had given her.

"Don't you worry, Mom," said Farticus, always the optimist. "We'll be okay."

"HELP!!" came a scream from outside.

Farticus and his mother rushed outdoors to see an old man trying to fend off the snapping jaws of a **three-metre crocodilus**.

"What the . . . ?" gulped Mrs Sandals. "Well, that's something you don't see every day."

Farticus rushed to the man's aid.

"**Farticus! No!**" his mother yelled after him.

CHAPTERUS FIVE

LOVE AND CROCODILUS

The old man had a rope in one hand. He tried to lasso the crocodilus's jaw as it angrily lunged and snarled at him. The prehistoric beast was only inches away from biting the old man's hand off.

"He broke out of his cage," grumbled the old man as Farticus came up beside him.

Farticus glanced over the old man's shoulder to see an opened cage on wheels attached to a couple of draught horses.

"Is there anything I can do?" asked Farticus, **excited** and **terrified** at the same time.

"Yes, there is," answered the old man. "You can try to distract him while I try to hoop this rope around his snout."

As Farticus raised his hands and danced about on the spot to get the crocodilus's attention,

he let out an **enormous fart**. It rumbled like thunder, causing birds to flutter out of the nearby treetops.

"Woah," croaked the old man. "You must be nervous, kid!"

"You haven't done a big one like that in a long time!" shouted Farticus's mother, rushing inside to grab another snotus rag.

"LOOK!" gasped the old man.

Farticus turned to see that the crocodilus had

passed out. Farticus had, not surprisingly, stunned it with his **vile gas**.

Farticus explained his life-long smelly problem to the old man. It wasn't until after Farticus had helped him tie the unconscious crocodilus's snout and drag it back into its cage that he suddenly realized something: "Why are you still

standing?" said Farticus to the old man. "Didn't you **smell my fart?**"

"I haven't been able to smell anything all my life," grinned the old man. "I was born with a rare nose disease that prevents me from smelling. I breathe only from my mouth. And the condition's hereditary—my daughter has it as well."

Farticus followed the old man's gaze back to the front of the cage and carriage to see a girl about his age waving back. In all the commotion he hadn't noticed her. Farticus's heart skipped a beat. It was **love at first sight** ... (yeah, yeah, I know this part of the story is kind of gushy ... I promise I'll try to keep it as short as possible) ... and by the way the girl blushed, it looked as though she felt the same way for Farticus.

"This is my daughter, Rhina," said the old man, as she made her way over to join them.

Farticus farted as he shook Rhina's hand— thankfully it was silent—and thankfully she couldn't smell it.

"And I'm Sinus," said the old man. "Sinus Blockus! I transport wild animals to the Colosseum in Rome, for the gladiator events and . . . "

Sinus suddenly clapped his hands together.

"That's it!" he announced. "I've got a brilliant idea!"

"He's always got a brilliant idea," added Rhina to Farticus.

Again, Farticus's heart skipped a beat.

"I've wanted to change jobs for years!" Sinus

said, becoming more and more excited. "Hey, kid, do you have a job?"

"No," mumbled Farticus, embarrassed in front of Rhina.

"Would you like one? One that will even make you rich and famous?"

"Heck, yeah!" nodded Farticus.

"You're going to be a **gladiator!** And I'm going to be your manager slash trainer!"

CHAPTERUS SIX

BLACK DOG BRUTUS

It took one entire year before Farticus became an official gladiator. Sinus and Rhina moved in with Farticus and his mother a week after they'd met. Sinus continued his transporting job to support them all, but on his days off he would train Farticus to become a **lean, mean fighting machine**, a super swordsman who would one day have to fight other gladiators, wild animals and murderous criminals, sometimes to the death, all in the name of entertainment.

"Your farting is your **secret weapon**, but it should not be your only one," Sinus would preach every day. "One day you might have to rely on your own physical and mental strength, and be a true gladiator!"

Normally, men who were chosen to be gladiators

went to a gladiator school where they would be trained professionally. But because of Farticus's lethal farts, this couldn't happen. So Farticus knew that he had to work doubly hard and do everything exactly the way Sinus wanted him to.

Eventually Farticus got to his first fight, against a bulky, scar-faced criminal called **Black Dog Brutus**. The battle was staged in a small stadium in a town not too far from Rome. Black Dog had gained a reputation as a fierce, dirty fighter and was touted as the next big sensation in the gladiator world. After this battle Black Dog was

Cue the Farticus 8-month-training-to-be-a-gladiator montage! And don't forget the sporty-sounding soundtrack!

Januarius

Februarius

Martius

Aprilis

Maius

Junius

Julius and Augustus

meant to go to the Colosseum to entertain the Emperor—but Farticus put an end to all of that.

In just a few minutes, Farticus blew Black Dog away with a rip-burner of a fart that made his eyes sting and his knees buckle to the ground.

Within a blink of an eye, Farticus leaped into the air and butterfly kissed Black Dog with a cold-blooded single **hug to the throat**.

The news of Black Dog's demise travelled like

lightning around the empire. Farticus and his farts
became instantly famous—and it was around this
time that he was dubbed **Farticus Maximus!**

Farticus Maximus went on to fight and win
forty-three battles in a row over the next
two years, all of them in the grand arena of the
Colosseum. Not only did he become super rich, he
became known as **the people's gladiator**.

Yes, life was good for Farticus, Sinus and Rhina, whom he later married. It was even good for Farticus's mother, Helena. She made a fortune selling her orange-scented snotus rags to spectators prior to each of Farticus's battles.

After three years as a full-time gladiator, and with some coaxing from Rhina, his mother and even Sinus, Farticus worked out that they could all live comfortably on his earnings, and so he decided he would retire. He announced that the next fight would be his last.

And that brings us back to where we started in Chapterus One: right bang in the middle of Farticus's last battle.

It was the battle of all battles; even the emperor had come to watch **Farticus's final showdown**. The crowd chanted in waves,

"Long live Farticus Maximus! Long live Farticus Maximus!"

But of course, that was all before the ferocious

BLACK DOG BRUTUS

EVIL FANGIUS

GLUTEUS MUGIS

CRUELIUS IV

SEBASTIUS DELIRIUS

BIGGUS BUTTUS

HONKIUS ENORMUS

HAIRIUS MOLEUS

lion surprised Farticus, and in a horrible twist of fate clawed him in the stomach, slicing his intestines, and **preventing him from farting**.

Farticus struggled to pass even a hint of gas, and he couldn't knock the lion out. For the first time in his gladiator career he had to rely on his own strength. But as we all know, Sinus had luckily prepared him for a moment just like this.

With all his might Farticus kicked, punched and wrestled the big cat. The crowd gasped; some couldn't even look. Farticus grabbed the lion in a headlock. Blood was gushing out of Farticus's wound and he was getting weaker by the second. With one last humongous effort, Farticus summoned the power inside and tried to **squeeze out a ripper**. The pain was excruciating and the lion was relentless. For the next few moments Farticus saw his life flash by; he saw his mother, Sinus and Rhina, the love of his life.

"You can do it," she said. "Find the wind within, Farticus! Find the wind within!"

The crowd roared, snapping Farticus back to life. With Rhina's voice still echoing in his ears, he squeezed, he squirmed, and . . . suddenly:

BBBRRRRRRPPPPPPPP!!!!!!

He farted. It was the fart of all farts. Many
of the spectators nearby were blown off their
pews! And as for the lion, the beast had no chance.
It was immediately stunned off its feet, allowing
Farticus to inflict the final blow with a hug to
the heart. The crowd erupted into screams and
cheers as their stinky hero saluted them with a
victory wave before collapsing with a thud on the
bloody arena.

It was several months before Farticus recovered fully, but by then he was a free and very wealthy man. He had become a **living legend**. To commemorate all his achievements, the emperor made it a law that whenever one would fart, bigus or smallus, they were to say, "*Long live Farticus Maximus!*"

Which isn't a bad law, if you ask me!

Who am I, you ask again?

Well, I was Farticus's very first real fart victim, blown off my feet all those years ago. My name is Juniper Sandals, Farticus's brother, and this was my story.

II. BETTER OUT THAN IN!

Jack Sheedy sat in the back seat of his family's car and gazed out the window. He saw a guy dressed in a bad reindeer costume handing out flyers in front of a hardware store. His mind drifted to last Christmas...

"Mom, you're sitting here next to me, Izzy, you're next to Dad, Vicky, you, Paul and baby Josh can take these three chairs, and Jack, you can sit next to your grandfather."

"*Sir, yes, sir!*" joked Jack, who was used to his mother taking control, especially when it came to bringing the family together for Christmas lunch.

"Don't be smart!" snapped Jack's mom.

"Yes, listen to the General," whispered Jack's grandfather.

"I heard that!"

Jack grinned. He loved his Grandpa Cal. He'd always goof around and would always, without fail, break wind. In fact, Grandpa Cal was so **proud of his farts** he'd make sure he'd announce them to everyone, even to those who were offended or disgusted by them—which tended to be most people—except Jack. Jack was his grandfather's number-one fan, farts and all.

"Dad, could you say a little something, some sort of prayer before we eat," asked Jack's mom, as she placed the roast turkey on the table.

"How about two, four, six, eight, let's dig in and hope it's great."

Grandpa winked at Jack.

"C'mon, Dad! Be serious for once! It's Christmas day," pleaded Jack's mother. "Mom, can't you get him to . . ."

"Don't rope me in," croaked Jack's grandmother. "I've had to put up with him for fifty years!"

"Okay, okay," said Grandpa Cal. "I'll say a proper prayer. I'll be serious this time."

Jack knew better.

"Dear Lord," his grandfather started. "We give thanks for the feast we are about to have and for the abundance of love and joy that is shared around this table . . ."

"Oh, Dad, that's so beautiful," gushed Jack's mom.

"I'm not finished," coughed Grandpa Cal.

"Sorry, Dad."

"And we give thanks for the weather . . ."

Again, Jack caught his grandfather wink at him.

"We give thanks for the sunshine and the rain . . ."

Jack noticed his grandfather slightly raise his left leg and without warning **suddenly let one rip**—a solid fart that echoed loudly against the vinyl chair.

"And we give thanks to the wind . . ."

"Oh, Dad, that's disgusting!" protested Jack's mom.

"Oh Calvin, how could you?" groaned Jack's grandmother.

"That's so gross!" cringed Jack's older sister, Izzy.

"Hey, I haven't finished," smirked Grandpa Cal.

Jack's face beamed with pride.

"And we give thanks to thunder—magnificent, booming, thunderous thunder!"

And with that, Jack's grandfather **squeezed out another beauty**, twice as loud as the last one.

"Amen!" he added.

"Amen!" repeated Jack.

* * *

Jack glanced over to Izzy; she was also lost in thought, staring out of the car window. Jack's mom was up front in the passenger seat checking her makeup in a compact mirror, while his dad was mumbling about the traffic and the city's need for more public transport. Again, Jack was reminded of his Grandpa Cal . . .

"So, what number do we take, Jack boy?"

"Number sixteen, Grandpa," answered Jack. "Here it is now!"

Jack and his grandfather hopped on to the bus and took a seat a couple of rows behind the driver. There were only a few other passengers on board.

"Thanks for wanting to come with me to the game, Grandpa," said Jack.

"I wouldn't miss it for the world, kid. Hope the Tigers win for us today!"

At the next stop a group of elderly women boarded the bus.

"Hello, ladies," greeted Grandpa Cal. "Lovely day for an outing!"

Some of the women nodded and smiled back at Jack's granddad.

"Off to play bingo or bowls, or to a walking stick convention I suspect," said Grandpa Cal.

"Maybe you should join them. That's more your speed, isn't it, Grandpa?"

"Hey, don't be cheeky!"

"Um, excuse me, young man," said one of the elderly women, tapping Jack on the shoulder. "Do you know the street before Green Street on this route?"

"Um, well, I think it's . . . "

"Smith Street!" blurted Grandpa Cal. "Or it could be Bell Street . . . no, no, it's not Bell, it's . . . now, let me think . . . "

Jack watched his grandfather squint his eyes and bite his bottom lip with his extra-white false teeth as he racked his brain for the street's name.

He also noticed the way he wriggled and squirmed in his seat. Jack panicked—this didn't look good. He could guess what was about to happen and before he could say, "*Sorry, we don't know, maybe that other passenger might!*" it was too late.

Grandpa Cal farted.

"Holy Mother of God, I think we just ran over a toad!" he joked.

Jack chuckled nervously. The lady and all her friends looked at one another aghast, but were too polite to say anything. That was, until Jack's grandfather farted again—three times!

"Woah, there goes an entire family of toads!" smirked Grandpa Cal. "Hey, driver, take it easy or I'll have to report you for cruelty to animals!"

"Well, I never!" cried the lady. "Please try to restrain yourself, sir!"

"It's not me! It's the driver, madam—all those poor toads on the road."

Again, Grandpa Cal farted.

"My mistake. They weren't toads. It was my pet duck in my back pocket!"

And if that wasn't enough, Jack's grandfather let another one rip.

"Settle down, duck!"

At the next stop, the elderly women stormed off the bus in utter disgust.

"Hey, ladies, you know **it's better out than in!**" Grandpa Cal shouted out after them.

* * *

Jack hopped out of the car, and with his family made his way toward the church. He jiggled his tie and collar. He had never worn a suit before. When the Sheedys approached the entrance they were greeted by grieving relatives and friends. Jack watched his mother burst into tears as she was hugged by her sister. He later caught sight of his school teacher, Miss Peters, in the crowd. He was touched to see her there. Once again, Grandpa Cal popped into his head . . .

"So, what's Miss Peters like?"

"What do you mean, Grandpa?" asked Jack.

"Well, is she all right on the eyes or what?"

"Grandpa!" scoffed Jack. "She's okay, I guess. I don't know."

Jack and his grandfather made their way into Jack's classroom and were greeted by Miss Peters.

"Va va voom! She's not half bad," Grandpa Cal whispered offside to Jack.

Jack rolled his eyes.

"Okay, everyone, put your pencils down, please!" announced Miss Peters. "We have a very special guest today, Jack's grandfather. He's here to talk about when he was a young man, a soldier at war. Make him feel very welcome!"

Everyone clapped loudly as Grandpa Cal took a step forward.

"Thanks, boys and girls. It's a real honour to be here today," he croaked. "I don't often talk about my time as a soldier because it still cuts very deep with me emotionally. All you need to know is that there are no winners in war."

One of Jack's classmates, Kevin Dodd, shot up his hand.

"Were you ever in any battles? Did you shoot or kill anyone? And what gun did you use?" he asked enthusiastically.

"Well, lad . . . ," said Grandpa Cal. "I can tell that you're the type of kid that'd like to hear the gruesome stuff. So I'm going to tell you."

"Yes!" hissed most of the boys in Jack's class.

"There was one battle I'll never forget," sighed Grandpa Cal. "It was a shootout to the very end and . . . "

Grandpa Cal paused as if he were lost for words. He was swaying from foot to foot and **jutting out his bottom** from side to side. Jack gulped. He knew that this could only mean one thing.

"... and fortunately," continued Grandpa Cal. "I had a machine gun and popped off a dozen bullets in a second ... "

This was it. Jack winced as Grandpa Cal proceeded to **fart several times in a row**.

Pop! Pop! Pop! Pop! Pop! Pop!

The class erupted into laughter. Miss Peters almost fell off her chair.

"They couldn't stop me!"

Grandpa Cal was on a roll. He farted some more: **Pop! Pop! Pop! Pop! Pop!**

Kevin Dodd leaned over to Jack and declared that his grandfather was the coolest granddad ever! Jack smiled. He already knew that.

* * *

Jack really wasn't listening to what the priest was saying about his grandfather. Instead he just stared at Grandpa Cal's coffin in a daze. Sobs and sniffles bounced off the cold stone church walls as one by one members of Jack's family got up

to speak about Grandpa Cal. Finally, it was Jack's turn. He shuffled up to the microphone, which was centred in the front of the altar.

He had written a speech the night before, but as he reached for it in his pocket he heard himself say, "What am I doing? He wouldn't want this. There's only one thing I can do."

Jack took the microphone out of its stand and pointed it toward his butt.

You can guess what happened next.

BBBRRRRRRPPPPPPPP!!!!!!!

Everyone gasped in horror—especially the priest.

"What do you think you're doing?" he growled.

"Well," said Jack with a grin, "**it's better out than in!**"

Jack turned to the coffin and whispered:

"I love you, Grandpa."

III.
MRS DEADLY GAS

"Ben, how was school?" asked my mom as I walked into her hairdressing salon. "Have you made some new friends?"

She was colouring an old woman's grey hair.

"Yeah," I mumbled, still not believing what had happened today.

I walked through to the back door of the salon that led to our apartment, collapsed on the couch and sighed.

Woah, what an unbelievably freaky day! Who would've thought that being the new kid at school would turn out to be so bizarro?

My friends at my old school will never believe me in a gazillion years when I call 'em tonight and tell 'em all about it ...

There I was this morning, before the first bell rang, shooting some hoops with three boys I sit next to in class. It was only my fourth day at Milton College and I was still getting to know everyone.

"No way! I don't believe it!" croaked Marty, a geeky-looking kid with tiny ears, big glasses and a squeaky voice.

"You gotta be kidding!" said Johnno, a hard core fan of world championship wrestling and truck drag racing.

"**We're all gonna die today!**" gasped Michael Tubble, Tubs for short.

I turned to see what they were staring at: a

very large woman was making her way through the school gates.

"What's going on?" I asked. "Who is she?"

"Tha … tha … that's **Mrs Deadly Gas!**" stuttered Tubs, before scampering off like a frightened rabbit.

"Mrs who?"

"Mrs Pegagus, she's an emergency teacher," said Marty. "Or Mrs Deadly Gas, as she's better known."

"Or more like *Mrs Her-farts-will-kill-you!*" added Johnno.

"You're not serious?" I chuckled.

Johnno grabbed hold of my shirt and yanked me in only inches away from his face.

"Hey," he hissed. "We've never been more serious. Read my lips new kid:

HER FARTS WILL KILL YOU!"

Marty pulled Johnno away.

"Settle down Johnno!" he said stepping in between us. "Sorry, Ben, Johnno didn't mean to

grab you like that. He's just scared—we all are. Look!"

Marty pointed over my shoulder. All the kids in the schoolyard were now running to get out of Mrs Deadly Gas's path.

"Let me explain the situation here," added Marty. "Last year a student by the name of Jordy Jones was **seriously hurt** by one of Mrs Pegagus's farts—and was rushed to hospital."

I snorted and stopped myself from laughing out loud. Johnno glared at me. Geez, this was serious. Marty continued.

"Jordy now goes to my cousin's school and I've heard he's never been the same since. Not since he was **blown away by her toxic gases**."

"Toxic gases?" I repeated. "Enough to hurt someone?"

"Yeah!" jumped in Johnno. "He's not making this up—it's totally for real! Tell him Marty! You're the brains in this school. Explain it to him."

"Well, Ben," sighed Marty. "Everyone farts at least fifteen times a day. A lot of the times we don't even know it. We just do it. It's a human thing. Come to think of it, it's also an animal thing."

I caught Mrs Deadly Gas moving closer toward us and now was wondering if I should be **seriously worried** or not. Marty was on a roll.

"Our farts are made of a mixture of gases—nitrogen, carbon dioxide, methane, and hydrogen sulphide."

How did he know all this?

" . . . it's the hydrogen sulphide that's the killer. It's the smelly gas," he added. "And from my own personal research I've worked out that Mrs Pegagus probably has an abnormally humongous amount of hydrogen sulphide in her farts. I calculated her gases have the same potency as that of twelve thoroughbred stallions all popping off at the same time!"

"We gotta split!" yelled Johnno. "She's almost here!"

Before I knew it I was chasing after Marty and Johnno.

We sprinted for a couple of minutes and ended up in the library.

"What's going on? What's the meaning of you bursting in like this?" growled Mrs Cherry, the librarian.

"Um ... well ... "

I was going to make up some fake reason for us all when I was surprised to hear Johnno tell her the truth:

"We're just getting away from Mrs Deadly ... I mean, Mrs Pegagus!"

"What?! She's here today!?" squealed Mrs Cherry, her face suddenly turning an off-white colour. "I've gotta go!"

Within seconds she was gone.

"See! Told ya it's for real!" said Johnno. "**Even the teachers are afraid!**"

"But I don't get it," I said. "I mean, how did the

actual fart hurt Jordy? And if Mrs Deadly Gas's gas is so dangerous to everyone why would the school still hire her?"

"You raise some good points," said Marty. "Allow me to explain where we last left off ... "

Marty took in a deep breath.

"The story goes ... " he began, "that Jordy was called up to join Mrs Pegagus at her desk at the front of the class—to do some sort of reading test with her."

"And then suddenly she let one **huge mother of a smelly explosion** rip!" interrupted Johnno.

"No! It didn't happen like that at all!" snapped Marty. "It was a slow buildup. I heard that Mrs Pegagus's nose and eyes began to twitch and blink all funny like, followed by uncontrollable hiccupping and burps and then ..."

"What?"

"And then ... *phooph!*"

"Phooph?"

"Yeah, *phooph*—that was the sound. It *wasn't* a rip-roaring monster fart. Nope, Mrs Pegagus had squeezed out a **silent but violent** one, an SBV—the deadliest of all farts. And poor Jordy got the brunt of it. His face turned lime green and he just keeled over—he fainted. Some said he was even unconscious. Everyone else in class was hit seconds later by the killer stench, but luckily they could get out—heaps of 'em threw up outside."

"What happened to Jordy?" I asked.

"Well, luckily by the time they got him to hospital he was breathing normally again. The doctors said he had a lack of oxygen to his brain and that ..."

"Yeah, it was the same as if he were drowning in a pool ..." Johnno interrupted again. "But not in water—in **a cloud of stink!**"

"Yeah, that's basically what happened," nodded Marty. "And to answer your question about why the school continues to hire her if her wind is so dangerous ... well, she wasn't blamed for it!"

"Why?"

"Because the air conditioning system in the school was acting up at the time and Jordy's passing out was blamed on the stale gases from air conditioning vents—and not Mrs Pegagus's fart."

Woah! Toxic gas? Killer stench? Cloud of stink? This was full on. I had never heard anything like it before in my entire life.

"Marty! Johnno!"

It was Tubs. He rushed over to us, his cheeks all rosy and flushed.

"You're not gonna believe it!" he panted heavily. "I just found out that Mr Graham is sick today!"

Mr Graham was our teacher.

"Oh mother of thunderpants!" gasped Johnno. "That means **we have Mrs Deadly Gas!**"

We all stood there stunned.

"All we can hope," said Marty with a grim look on his face, "is that she hasn't recently eaten the best fart-making food on the planet: **bean and cabbage casserole**—that's what she had for lunch on the day she almost killed Jordy."

For most of the morning everyone in class sat at their desks frozen with fright. No one wanted to disturb Mrs Pegagus in any way for fear of causing her to release her killer gas.

We all quietly and busily worked on the assignments Mr Graham left for us, occasionally glancing up at each other, desperately hoping that none of us would end up being Mrs Deadly Gas's next victim.

"*Hello, students and teachers,*" echoed our principal's voice over the speakers. "*As you can see, the heavens have opened up and the rain doesn't look like it's going to stop. So, lunch today will be had indoors by all, in your classrooms. Thank you.*"

A few moments later the bell rang—it was

officially lunchtime.

"I don't believe it," whispered Marty, as we all made our way to get our lunches from our school bags.

"What?"

"Look!"

I turned to see Mrs Deadly Gas pull the lid off a plastic container.

"**Holy fart-maker!**" coughed Johnno. "It's bean and cabbage casserole!"

"Quick, we have to do something," panicked Tubs.

"I've got an idea!" said Marty. "Ben, you gotta go and swap your lunch with Mrs Pegagus. We gotta stop her from eating or doing something that may cause her to let one rip!"

"But why does it have to be me?" I asked.

"Because you're the new kid and she doesn't know you," Johnno piped in. "If any of us did it she'd know something was up. Now go!"

"C'mon, Ben," urged Marty.

"Yeah, Ben, do it for all of us!" pleaded Tubs.

Talk about pressure. I agreed to do it.

"Um, excuse me, Mrs Deadly . . . , I mean, Mrs Pegagus, I'm new at this school and I couldn't help notice that you're having bean and cabbage casserole for lunch . . . "

Mrs Deadly Gas was just about to take her first mouthful. I was really nervous standing so close to her, but I kept going:

"And . . . I was wondering if we could swap lunches. You can have my really tasty chicken sandwich if you like. Please have it!"

Mrs Deadly Gas politely said, "No thanks." In fact, she said that she loved bean and cabbage casserole so much that she had had it for the past four days straight. I shot a panicked look back at Marty, Tubs and Johnno.

"**i think we're in big trouble**," I mouthed back at them.

Suddenly I noticed Mrs Deadly Gas's face

begin to twitch and her eyes blink rapidly. She also started to hiccup and burp uncontrollably.

"Are you okay?" I asked her.

She didn't answer me.

Oh no. This didn't look good. My heart was racing. I didn't want to end up in hospital like that Jordy kid. And I didn't want anyone else to get hurt either. There was only one thing I could do:

"EVERYONE, RUN FOR YOUR LIVES!" I screamed rushing toward the door. "SHE'S GOING TO LET ONE RIP!"

I bolted out of the classroom, through the corridor, and out into the rain.

But hang on! Where was everyone else? Why hadn't they followed me? I waited. Oh no. This is bad, real bad. Had everyone been blown away by Mrs Deadly Gas's deadly gas? And **was i the sole fart survivor?**

I shuffled reluctantly inside, and, holding my breath, I poked my head back into the classroom.

"ARRRGHH HA! HA! HA! HA!"

Everyone was laughing hysterically—even Mrs Deadly Gas was in fits. What was going on? Marty, Tubs and Johnno were laughing so hard that they had tears in their eyes.

"Good on ya, Ben!" came a voice from behind.

It was our teacher Mr Graham. Now I was really confused. Mrs Deadly Gas came over and patted me on the shoulder.

"That was priceless!" she chortled. "Your reaction was fantastic!"

"What!? What d'ya mean?" I croaked. "What's going on?"

Mr Graham got Marty to explain everything to me in front of everyone. He explained how it was all made up—from the story about Mrs Pegagus and Jordy, to everyone running out of her way in the schoolyard to Mrs Cherry's reaction in the library, to . . . well, everything. It was all staged as **one big joke** to officially welcome me to Milton College.

"You all went to that much trouble just to welcome me here?" I stuttered, still in shock.

"Yes," said Mr Graham. "We pride ourselves on doing this to all our new students. We even have a reputation for it. It's a wonder you hadn't heard about it before you got here."

"No, I hadn't," I shrugged. What else could I say? "Um, thanks," I coughed.

Everyone gave me three cheers for being a good sport and again officially welcomed me to Milton College.

See! Bizarro! Yep, my friends at my old school will never believe me.

"Okay, you!" announced my mom, bouncing into the apartment. "I've locked up the salon early tonight because I'm in the mood to make us a real home-cooked meal."

"Sweet," I mumbled, still lying on the couch in a daze. "What are we having?"

"Something I've wanted to make for a while: bean and cabbage casserole!"

73

75

V.
PULL MY FINGER

"Get out of the way, geek!"

That's me. Geek. Or nerd. Or brainiac. Or bookhead. And that was Rodney Galloway, shoving me into the lockers as he and some of the other boys in my class barrel down the corridor.

"For the hundredth time this year, my name is Miles J. T. Greville," I shout after him, realizing that that was probably a totally geeky thing to say.

When I join my friends—yes, other geeks, Roland and Marvin—at the lockers, I'm overcome by melancholy: see, I've just done it again! What kid says "overcome by melancholy"? Okay, I'm *sad*, for the non-geeks among you.

"Hey, Miles! Are you ready for our five-minute oral presentations today? Are you still going to talk about **famous rock formations** of the world?" Roland asks enthusiastically.

"Yes," I mumble, throwing my school bag on top of the lockers.

"I can't wait!" adds Marvin. "The fact that Miss Levine gave us an open slate to discuss anything we want to, like my love for opera sopranos of the twentieth century ... well, that's just pure bliss."

"Is it, Marvin?" I say sarcastically. "Is it pure bliss? Can't it just be ... well, good, or cool even?"

"Pardon?"

I catch Marvin shooting a confused look at Roland.

"Well, I think I'm going to begin my talk about possible life forms on other planets with a photograph of a real-life alien that was captured by the US army in the 1950s," says Roland, shrugging off my cold response to Marvin.

"That's great," I mumble and sigh loudly.

We begin to make our way to class.

"What's wrong?" asks Marvin. "Do I detect that someone is a little low today?"

"No, Marvin!" I snap and stop to face him. "How about not *detecting* but instead just *noticing*, or *seeing* that I'm a little melancholy, I mean, *sad* ... the way most people would say it!"

Marvin and Roland are speechless.

"Sorry," I add. "I didn't mean to jump down your throat, I just, well, do you ever wonder why we're **not popular** with the other kids?"

"Not really," croaks Marvin.

I detect, I mean, *see*, that he's frightened that I might snap at him again.

"Doesn't it bug you both that we're always going to be known as **geeks?**" I continue. "And well, geeks are never popular, are they?"

"Who cares about being popular when you're super intelligent?" boasts Roland.

"I know, but being super intelligent doesn't get you noticed, does it?"

"Yes, it does!" chimes Marvin. "If you're a brilliant writer or a scientist you're sure to capture the attention of the Nobel Prize committee and ..."

"No, I don't mean that," I cut Marvin off. "I mean to be noticed by everyday people, other kids!"

"I get noticed by Rodney Galloway and his gang of buffoons most days of the week!" says Roland, pulling up his sleeve to show a bruise on his arm. "He did this to me yesterday after school. All I said was, 'Rodney, it's very hot today. I hope you and your friends are wearing SPF 30 or higher sunscreen.' And then he replied, 'How about this for SPF 30?' And he thumped me!"

I felt for Roland. No one deserves that, not even a geek. But my friends weren't getting me.

"All I'm saying is," I press on, "is that it would be nice to be noticed by other kids, not bullies like Rodney Galloway and his friends. You know, just a friendly smile from someone . . .'"

"From whom?" Marvin asks.

Right then it happens—as if on cue. Maddie O'Sullivan and her friends breeze by. I can't take my eyes off her. She's probably the **most beautiful girl** in the entire school. Her long, silky red hair is swaying from side to side, as if it's in slow motion—like one of those shampoo commercials. She smiles and I'm finding it hard to breathe. I try to smile in her direction, desperate to catch her eye. But she doesn't notice me. It's as if I'm wearing some sort of invisibility cloak. She marches right past me.

A few moments later I turn back to Marvin and Roland. They're shaking their heads.

"What?" I ask.

"So, that's who you want to be noticed by?" they say in unison.

"No, yes, um . . . well," I stutter.

It's no use. My friends have caught me out. This was the reason for my melancholy—I mean sadness. Someone like Maddie O'Sullivan would never notice someone like me, a geek.

"That explains it," coughs Marvin, all smug-like. "But you know she likes you-know-who?"

"Who?" I ask.

Marvin points ahead. I look up and see Maddie laughing and chatting with Rodney Galloway. He and his friends are showing off, if you call getting one another in headlocks and corking thighs showing off.

"My sister, who's friends with Maddie's sister, said that Rodney asked Maddie to go out with him, and she said she'd get back to him at the end of the week," Marvin exclaims.

A week. Hmm? That's all the time I have to become popular and win the attention of the girl of my dreams. Yeah, right. Who am I kidding!?

Seven hours later and I'm still feeling melancholy, sorry, *sad*. I'm on a train heading home, thinking of a million things: Maddie, Rodney, Marvin and Roland, geeks not being popular, my oral presentation on rock formations of the world—which by the way, I did well in.

For a moment there, when I was in the middle of talking about metamorphic rocks, I thought I had caught Maddie **smiling at me**. Maybe she was laughing at me? I know Rodney and his friends were.

"Pull my finger! Go on!"

I snap out of my thoughts and look up to see that at the end of the carriage a group of schoolboys about my age are messing around. Most of the adult passengers on board are not impressed: they're pulling annoyed expressions while continuing to look busy with their newspapers, iPods or books.

"Come on! Pull my finger!" says one of the boys loudly, not concerned that the whole carriage can hear him.

Another boy obliges and pulls his finger.

BBBRRRRRRPPPPPPPP!!!!!!

I can't believe it. The boy just broke wind. Okay, farted, massively, in front of everyone. The boys are high-fiving each other and **laughing hysterically**.

An elderly lady sitting next to the boys leaves her seat and makes her way to my end of the carriage.

"Rude!" she mumbles.

"Pull my finger!" the boy says again.

Again he lets one rip at the exact same time that one of his friends tugs at his finger. Part of me wants to laugh and part of me thinks it's imbecilic … but strangely, most of me is intrigued.

I keep watching the boys, who, by the way, remind me of Rodney Galloway and his gang, and I notice how the pull-my-finger boy is getting a lot of attention from his friends. He's definitely popular. Suddenly, I have a theory: doing stupid things that make your friends laugh equals being popular.

I think about this all the way home.

* * *

It's the next day, and I'm back at school. I'm shuffling into class; the first period of the day. It's math and our teacher, Mr Jones, isn't here yet. I sit at a desk at the front of the classroom, next to Marvin and Roland.

"Hey, bookheads," snarls Rodney Galloway, swaggering in. "Did you do my homework last night? Give me your answers!"

Marvin pulls out his math homework. He's

about to hand it over to Rodney. This is totally unjust. Okay, what would a non-geek say? **This totally sucks**. Yes, this sucks! And it needs to be stopped, right now.

"Don't give it to him!" I say to Marvin.

Marvin and Roland's eyes pop out of their heads.

"What did you say?" growls Rodney.

"I said he shouldn't give it to you!"

"And why not?!"

Rodney clasps his hand around my neck. I am now having second thoughts. He's going to kill me. I wonder if Maddie is watching this. I wonder if she's impressed by Rodney's manliness. Or my unmanliness?

"I said, WHY NOT?" repeats Rodney, as he squeezes his fingers deeper into my throat.

It's hard to breathe. I'm frightened. I'm so scared right now that I want to go to the washroom. Actually, I want to fart.

Suddenly. An idea.

"He can't give you his homework," I squeak. "Because I want you to **pull my finger!**"

I raise my right hand and stick out my forefinger.

Rodney lets go of his grip. Ah, oxygen! I can breathe again.

"What?" Rodney asks.

"I said I want you to pull my finger before you take Marvin's homework!"

Rodney is suspicious.

"Okay then," he says.

He tugs at my finger and I, thankfully, **let one rip**. It's louder than I think it will be.

Everyone—they are all watching at this stage—cracks up laughing. But it's Rodney who's most amused.

"Sweet!" he says, putting out his hand to give me a high five.

He slaps my hand. Wow! My first high five—and it feels extraordinary . . . cool, even.

"**Do it again!**" orders Rodney.

"Yeah, do it again!" echo some of the others.

Rodney pulls my finger. I fart. Perfect. Everyone is laughing, except for Marvin and Roland; they're in complete shock. But I don't care. Everyone notices me. And by everyone, I mean Maddie O'Sullivan. She's laughing with everyone else.

Rodney's friends all want a turn.

"Sorry I'm late everyone. Back to your desks!"

Phew! It's Mr Jones. I wasn't sure I had any more farts left in me.

"Hey, Greville!" whispers Rodney. "Come and **sit next to us!**"

I can't believe it. Nor can Marvin and Roland, especially when I pick up my books and join Rodney and his friends at the back of the classroom. Everyone is looking. And by everyone, I mean Maddie O'Sullivan.

Fast-forward three days: It's morning recess, Friday, and life is good. In the past four days I have become, against all odds, popular. Okay, most of the students still don't know my real name. Everyone has come to call me simply **Fart Boy**. I can live with that ... well, for now. Farting on cue isn't as easy as you might think.

But as long as it keeps me in the spotlight, I can't complain. And by spotlight, I mean on Maddie O'Sullivan's radar. And by the way, she rejected Rodney Galloway before first class earlier this morning. So, that's where I'm off to now: to finally talk to the girl of my dreams. And I'm going to ask her to be **my girlfriend**. Yep, being popular, as you can probably tell, has made me a whole lot more confident and self-assured. Marvin and Roland call it being obnoxious and a big-head. But what would they know? And who cares if they're not talking to me! Just because I said to them it wasn't good for my new-found image to be seen with geeks. They're just jealous.

Okay. This is it. I have Maddie in my sights. She's

just left her friends to grab something out of her locker. Good. She's on her own. This is the perfect time to make my move.

Relax. Play it easy. Cool. My heart feels like it's in my throat. And my lips are so dry! I wish I'd had a drink before doing this.

"Um ... hello, Maddie!" I stutter.

She turns. And ... yes, she smiles at me. Good start.

"Yes," she says.

"Um, I'm not sure if you know who I am ... "

"Of course I do!"

Of course she does. Why wouldn't she know me? I'm Mr Popular, the one and only Fart Boy. There's no way she could've missed me all week. All right, it's now or never.

"Um, would you like to **go out with me** ... um, you know in a sort of girlfriend–boyfriend ... um, sort of capacity?"

I swear, my heart has just stopped. Did I

seriously say it?

Maddie is blushing.

"Um . . ." she stutters.

I want to say something, to stop this really awkward moment. But I can't think of anything.

"Look," she spits out. "To be honest, if you had asked me on Monday afternoon, I probably would've said yes. But **no, not now**."

What? I think back to Monday. Nothing. Why Monday? I was a geek on Monday, and I've only been popular since Tuesday. I say this to Maddie.

"And you didn't even know I existed on Monday!" I add.

"Yes, I did!" she says. "Your 'Rock Formations of the World' presentation was brilliant. My dad's a geologist. And I hope to be one someday, too."

My jaw dropped. **She's a geek** like me! She's more amazing than I have ever imagined. I scramble for something else to say.

"So, you don't care that I can fart on cue? That

I'm popular?"

I realized as I was saying it that that sounded pretty lame.

"Please!" Maddie scoffs. "I might've laughed the first time you did that pull-my-finger stunt. But by the third time, I was over it. It's **kind of childish** and, well, I wouldn't want to go out with anyone who's that ... well, imbecilic! That's why I also said no to Rodney."

Now I know what you're thinking. That last comment must be killing me. But it isn't. I can't be happier! Sure, I know my chances are blown with Maddie, but she's just confirmed one thing to me. It's okay for me to be me—a super-intelligent, not-at-all-popular geek.

To tell you the truth, I was already a little over being Fart Boy myself. So, this only leaves me with one thing to do.

I look down at my watch. There are only two minutes left of morning recess. I run. I run all the way to the library and make my way to the non-fiction section and there they are: Marvin and Roland.

"Hi," I say.

They both give me looks as if to say, what are you doing here?

"Pull my finger!" I say.

"We're not into your toilet humour, thank you very much," snaps Marvin. "How about you ask your new friends, Rodney and his moronic pals!"

"Just pull it!" I insist.

"No!" snaps Roland. "Just leave us alone, Miles. Remember you don't want to be seen with any geeks!"

"Go on, pull my finger! I'm not leaving until you do!"

I shove my finger close to Marvin's face. Reluctantly he tugs at it.

As he does, I say, 'I'm very sorry for saying what I said to you both . . . and for being such an **idiot**

all week. You are my best friends, and I should never have treated you like that."

I now point my finger at Roland.

"Pull my finger, please!"

As Roland yanks at my finger I continue to say, "I hope that you will be able to forgive me. Because I think that we geeks should stick together."

Marvin and Roland remain silent. I turn to walk away.

"Hey!" shouts Marvin.

"Yeah, hold on!" echoes Roland.

I turn back to face them.

"We forgive you, Fart Boy!"

VI.

Far ~~Cartoons~~

aka famous movies with a stinky twist!

KING PONG

HAPPY FART

MARY POP-OFTENS

HARRY POTTY VERSUS VOLDERFART

GONE WiTH THE WiND
(THIS ONE IS FOR YOUR GRANDPARENTS)

GASSiE

FLATUDANCE

(THIS ONE IS FOR YOUR PARENTS)

FARTLOOSE

(ANOTHER ONE FOR YOUR FOLKS)

FARTING NEMO

RATAPOOEY

JURGASIC PARK

PiCHOKEiO

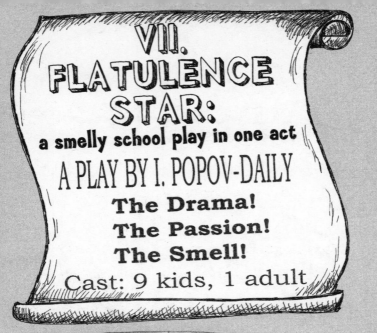

VII.
FLATULENCE STAR:
a smelly school play in one act
A PLAY BY I. POPOV-DAILY
The Drama!
The Passion!
The Smell!
Cast: 9 kids, 1 adult

To perform this play you will need a cast of you, eight of your friends and one adult.

CAST

Host Johnny

Touchdown Dude

Stinko

Fluffia

Vile

Matt McGuiness

Jennifer Doozey

Boom Boom Benny Manaro

Woman (Adult)

Official Flatulence Spokesperson (OFS)

A stage is set up to represent a TV studio: vibrant lights, a raised podium upstage with microphone on a stand, and a huge banner draped at the back that reads FLATULENCE STAR. To the left of the stage sit FOUR JUDGES, three boys and one girl. Offstage we hear a booming adult voice come across the speakers:

"PUT YOUR HANDS TOGETHER AND MAKE SOME NOISE FOR YOUR HOST, JOHNNY P. U. TRID!"

The audience cheer and clap loudly as HOST JOHNNY runs to the centre of the stage.

HOST JOHNNY: Thank you! Thank you! You're so kind! Welcome to "Flatulence Star," the show that aims to blow you away every week with amazing rip-roaring performances, and ultimately uncover this year's Flatulence Star! We're now down to the final three, the serious bottom end of the competition. But before we bring out our contestants, let's give a hot-air welcome to our judges: Touchdown Dude, Stinko, Fluffia, and Vile.

Audience applause. Judges wave.

HOST JOHNNY: Thanks, judges—we'll be hearing from you soon. Okay, let's get on with the show. This week "anything goes" is the theme, which means it's up to our contestants to choose whatever form of wind-breaking method they want. So, up first is a guy that the country fell in love with from day one. Yes, you know who I'm talking about. Give it up for Matt McGuiness as he performs his very own composition, Armpit Symphony!

The audience cheer as MATT McGUINESS makes his way to the centre of the stage. Matt is wearing a tanktop that reads, My Armpit Rules! Matt proceeds to lick his right hand a few times, cup his left armpit and do "armpit farts" into the microphone. He does this for up to thirty seconds. He stops, stands aside from the microphone and bows. Again, the audience cheer.

HOST JOHNNY: Matt McGuiness, everyone! Nice one, Matt! But let's see what the judges thought. Touchdown Dude?

TOUCHDOWN DUDE: Look, Matt, you know I like you, but I just didn't feel it. And you had some major pitch problems in the middle of that. Sorry, but that stunk!

STINKO: Yeah, Matt, I've got to agree with Touchdown Dude. I was expecting a little more from you this week. To be honest, that was a train wreck.

The audience boo and hiss at Stinko's last comment. Host Johnny looks to the female judge on the panel, FLUFFIA, for her thoughts.

FLUFFIA: Matt, how did you feel through that?

MATT: Um, I felt good.

FLUFFIA: Well, darling, that's all a true wind breaker can ever want. You gave it your best, and for that I thank you very much. Well done, darling.

HOST JOHNNY: And finally, Vile...

VILE: Well... I loved it!

The audience cheer.

VILE: I don't know what Tweedledee and Tweedledum at the other end of this table are talking about. That to me was a superstar performance. That's what great-sounding flatulence is all about! Fartastic, Matt!

Again the audience cheer. Matt exits stage left.

HOST JOHNNY: If you want to keep Matt in the competition, then you know what to do. SMS "MATT" to the number that's on your screen now. Okay, let's bring out our next gassy finalist. She's loud, she's proud, she's irreverent, she's... Jennifer Doozey!

JENNIFER DOOZEY strolls on stage carrying a chair. Everyone gives the young girl a rousing welcome. Jennifer places the chair in the centre of the stage. She holds a whoopee cushion up to the audience, blows it up, and places it gently on the chair. She motions for Host Johnny to position his microphone by the whoopee cushion. Jennifer takes a theatrical pause, and as the drum rolls she drops bottom first on to the whoopee cushion:

BBBRRRRRRPPPPPPPP!!!!!!

The audience jump to their feet in hysterics. Jennifer repeats her whoopee cushion act three more times before taking her final bow.

HOST JOHNNY: Give it up one more time for Jennifer Doozey! Judges what did you make of that? Fluffia?

FLUFFiA: Now that's what I'm talkin' 'bout! That is some of, if not *the* best, whoopee cushion action we've seen in a long, long time! You go, girl!

STiNKO: I echo Fluffia. Jennifer, that was the absolute best we've seen from you. You are born to simulate farts, sweetheart. I closed my eyes in the middle of that performance, and I swear it was real. It was raw. It was ripe. It was pure brilliance.

The audience cheer.

ViLE: Yep, you are a star, but I do have one criticism. What's with the tacky-looking plastic school chair? I would've liked to see a more stylish, hipper-looking chair. Perhaps even a stool. But otherwise, that was awesome.

HOST JOHNNY: Thanks, Vile. And finally, Touchdown Dude!

TOUCHDOWN DUDE: That was sublime, girl. What you did with that whoopee cushion . . . oh, Mama! The range was superb!

The audience begin to chant, "TOUCHDOWN! TOUCHDOWN! TOUCHDOWN!" Touchdown Dude stands up on his chair, swings his right arm in a circular motion several times, before pointing to Jennifer and shouting: **TOUCHDOWN!**

The audience jump to their feet and cheer loudly.

HOST JOHNNY: Well, Jennifer, you've got to be happy about that!

JENNIFER: Yeah, that's pretty awesome.

HOST JOHNNY: Well, folks, if you want to see more cracking and explosive performances like that one from Jennifer next week, get voting now!

Jennifer exits the stage.

HOST JOHNNY: Now we've come to our final performance of the show. This performer has come to shock us week in and week out. He's been dubbed the bad boy of the group. But we here can't get enough of him! Put your hands together for Boom Boom Benny Manaro!

BOOM BOOM BENNY saunters on stage. He lowers the microphone on the stand to the height of his waist. He turns his back to the audience, pulls his pants down, exposing his spiderman boxer shorts, and aims his bottom toward the mic.

There are gasps from some of the audience members, as they predict what might happen next.

WOMAN: STOP! STOP! DON'T YOU DARE!

A voice shouts from the back row. It's an adult, a woman. She storms toward the stage.

WOMAN: STOP! PULL YOUR PANTS UP RIGHT NOW, YOUNG MAN!

Boom Boom Benny does as he's told. He looks to Host Johnny and the judges; everyone is confused by this disruption. The woman stomps her way up on to the stage.

HOST JOHNNY: Um, can we help you? We're in the middle of a play here! Can someone please give this woman a microphone?

A boy runs on stage from the wings and hands a wireless microphone to the woman.

HOST JOHNNY: You were saying, Madam?

WOMAN: Enough is enough! I came here today to support kids in theatre, to see them display some sort of creativity and imagination. But instead I get this! This is nothing short of disgusting. There's nothing creative or imaginative about doing an entire play based on bodily functions. It's not witty or clever. It's juvenile! It's degrading and it lacks class. What about acting out a nice Shakespearian scene? Or a pleasant, classic children's story from Roald Dahl? Or a play about some important historical figure, like Benjamin Franklin perhaps? This is what you should aspire to. Not this sort of cheap and revolting toilet humour! I'm outraged by this farce and the world does not find—and excuse me for saying this because I detest this word—but the world does not find *farting* funny!

HOST JOHNNY: Well, okay, thanks.

WOMAN: That's it? That's all you've got to say on the subject?

HOST JOHNNY: No, but we usually leave the talking to our OFS.

WOMAN: OFS?

HOST JOHNNY: Yes, our Official Flatulence Spokesperson. I think I hear him coming now!

WOMAN: You do?

Suddenly the sound of trumpets heralding OFS's arrival blares loudly offstage. The OFS, a small boy dressed in a three-piece suit, marches on stage and takes his stand by the microphone. He unfolds a piece a paper that rolls out all the way down to his feet. He begins to read . . .

OFS: Dear fellow wind breakers and outraged woman. I speak for all those who have ever let one rip: this includes everyone from kings to little old ladies to cute toddlers to bus drivers and everyone else in between. But before I go on it's traditional that you, the audience, declare your support for the wind within. Every time you hear me say, *Hail to the Wind* I would like you to respond by blowing the biggest and loudest raspberry you possibly can. Let's have a practice run.

HAIL TO THE WIND!

Audience respond by blowing one loud raspberry:

BBBRRRRRRRPPPPPPPPP!!!!!!!

OFS: Okay, some of you got it, but I know we can be louder than that.

HAIL TO THE WIND!

Audience responds again:

BBBRRRRRRPPPPPPPP!!!!!!

OFS: Great! Now, Madam, while I respect your opinions, I strongly disagree with you and declare that for many of us, "popping off," "passing gas," "doing a fluffy," "tooting," or just plain old "farting" is funny. HAIL TO THE WIND!

Audience responds:

BBBRRRRRRPPPPPPPP!!!!!!

OFS: This does not mean that we lack a sophisticated sense of humour or intelligence. In fact we kids can often tell the difference between crassness and harmless goofiness. It's the grown-ups that often can't. HAIL TO THE WIND!

Audience responds:

BBBRRRRRRPPPPPPPP!!!!!!

OFS: We know it's considered not polite to "squeeze one out" when you're in the company of others, so please give us some credit. It's not like we're going to lose total control of our manners just because we like to laugh at fart jokes. HAIL TO THE WIND!

Audience responds:

BBBRRRRRRPPPPPPPP!!!!!!

OFS: But when we accidentally "let one loose" in public, I speak for us all when I say we're usually a little embarrassed, but most of all amused. Personally, it's the sound that cracks me up. HAIL TO THE WIND!

Audience responds:

BBBRRRRRRPPPPPPPP!!!!!!

OFS: I also must point out to you that many of the most revered writers of all time have written about farting. Literary legends like Cicero, Chaucer, Dante, Twain, Swift and yes, even Shakespeare, have written verses that at one point or another have, shall we say, *popped off* the pages! HAIL TO THE WIND!

Audience responds:

BBBRRRRRRPPPPPPPP!!!!!!

OFS: Maybe you're right, Madam, maybe we should consider doing a Shakespeare play. But wait! Perhaps we should do something from Roald Dahl, the legendary children's author you mentioned. Hmmm? Maybe we should stage his "The BFG" story and re-enact the Big Friendly Giant's love of farting, or *whiz-popping* as he calls it. Millions of children, me included, have laughed and enjoyed this story. HAIL TO THE WIND!

Audience responds:

BBBRRRRRRPPPPPPPP!!!!!!......

OFS: And let's not forget Benjamin Franklin, one of America's founding fathers, the man who discovered electricity, and whose face is on the American hundred-dollar bill. Yes, the same man who also had a lot to say about passing gas. Believe it or not, Madam, Benjamin Franklin wrote a letter to the Royal Academy of Medicine on the subject suggesting it was better for our health to break wind and fart proudly. HAIL TO THE WIND!

Audience responds:

BBBRRRRRRPPPPPPPP!!!!!!

OFS (*getting more worked up*): And what about all the millions of movie-goers who have had a good belly-laugh at classic wind-breaking scenes in movies like *Blazing Saddles, Austin Powers, Liar Liar, Back to School, Shrek* and *The Nutty Professor.* And don't even get me started on TV shows! HAIL TO THE WIND!

Audience responds:

BBBRRRRRRPPPPPPPP!!!!!!

OFS: And finally, passing gas has been around since the start of time and for many it will always be funny. In today's world of doom and gloom what's so bad about having a chuckle and finding a little joy in something that comes so naturally for every single one of us—including you, Madam.

HOST JOHNNY: Thank you OFS . . . so, Madam, there you have it. What have you got to say before we continue with our show?

MADAME: HAIL TO THE WIND!

Audience responds:

BBBRRRRRRPPPPPPPP!!!!!!!

Black out. End.

VIII. MY DAD, THE FART DOCTOR

"Time to go, birthday boy!"

"Yeah, I'm coming, Dad!"

Josh Hewitt tied up his shoes, slammed his bedroom door shut, and bounced downstairs. He couldn't wait to get going; turning eleven and getting to celebrate with his best friends at Extreme Water World wasn't the sort of thing that happened every day.

"So, you ready?" grinned Mr Hewitt waiting in

the hallway. "Your mother's already in the car. I think she's more excited than you are!"

"She's not going down the same slides with us!"

"So you've already said a million times!"

"And Dad . . . you're not going to talk about your job today, okay?" added Josh as he and his father closed the front door behind them.

"I said I'd try not to, didn't I? Besides, you told your friends that *I'm just a regular old doctor.* I don't know why you didn't tell them the truth. You know that I'm very proud to be a **gastroenterologist** and if anyone wants to know more, I'm always happy to talk to them about it!"

I know, thought Josh. *That's the problem.*

Josh and his parents made their way to pick up his friends. But first they needed to stop for gas. Josh trailed his dad up to the cash register—his mom wanted him to get some mints.

There was a long line of people paying for their

gas. Josh and his dad were four customers away from the counter. The man standing directly in front of them **suddenly broke wind**—loudly.

Everyone stopped, even the woman at the cash register; they shot the man a disgusted look.

"Sorry about that," said the man, looking a little embarrassed as he reached to grab some chewing gum and a can of orange fizz from the fridge.

"That's perfectly fine," said Josh's dad. "But if you suffer from **excessive flatulence**, I'd stay away from the chewing gum and fizzy drinks."

"Sorry?" said the man.

"Daaa-ad!" groaned Josh.

Mr Hewitt repeated himself.

"Well . . . to be honest," said the man, lowering his voice. "I do suffer from well, you know . . . "

"Constant *flatus*, which is the medical term for farts, from the Latin meaning 'the act of blowing,'" exclaimed Mr Hewitt.

Josh rolled his eyes.

"Um, yeah, are you a doctor or something?" asked the man.

"Yes, I'm a gastroenterologist," said Josh's dad. "Passing gas is my field ... or should that be bag? Gas bag, get it?"

Josh just shook his head.

"Yeah, I get it," said the man. "So, you were saying that I should stay away from chewing gum? Why?"

"When you chew quickly it causes you to take in a lot of air. This can lead to bloating of the colon and it turns the air inside into **potent gas**. And as for the can of fizzy orange you have in your hand, well, a lot of carbonated beverages have fructose in them. It's a type of sugar that the intestines have a hard time absorbing, so that can lead to ... "

"Flatus, eh?" said the man, appearing pleased to

have learned a new word.

"Exactly!" said Mr Hewitt.

* * *

"What took you guys so long?" asked Josh's
mother when they returned to the car.

Josh explained and his mother rolled her eyes.

"Don't blame me!" said Mr Hewitt, strapping on
his seat belt. "The man needed my help. He tooted
right in front of us! Talking about tooting, who
just **let one rip**? Josh?"

"It wasn't me!" snapped Josh, who had to admit
there was a pretty rotten smell in the car.

Josh's dad turned to his mother.

"Well it wasn't me, if that's what you think!" she
coughed. "Maybe it was you, Doctor? Flatulence is
your life, remember!"

Josh shook his head. Just once he wished he
could go through an entire day without hearing
about the gas we pass.

An hour later, he and his folks had picked up his

friends Pete, Mitch and Kenny. They had changed into their board shorts, and were now standing in line at Extreme Water World, waiting for their turn on the water slide called Mega Drop.

"This is going to be so awesome!" said Pete. "This is a cool party idea, Hewy!"

"Yeah, I thought it would be," said Josh, who was leading his friends in a long line of about thirty other excited kids and adults.

"Get a move on you guys!" grinned Mr Hewitt, who was also in line behind Josh and his friends. "I have the *need* for *speed!*"

"How fast do you think we can go down it?" asked Kenny, who, without warning, farted.

Josh's friends laughed.

"Nice one, Kenny!"

Josh could see that Kenny was **clearly embarrassed**.

"Sorry, Mr Hewitt," he said.

"That's okay! It's quite common for nerves

to cause flatulence. I have a lot of patients who suffer from the same condition."

"You do?" asked Kenny. "Josh said you were a doctor. What sort of doctor are you?"

"Dad!" yelled Josh, looking back over his shoulder.

"Hey, you! You're next!"

Josh had made it to the top of the slide. He had no time to stop his dad from telling his friends more about his job. The attendant was pressuring him to take off.

"I said, kid, you're next!"

Josh dived onto the slide, wondering all the way down what his father was saying to Kenny. When he made it to the bottom he waited for the others to follow. When they hopped out of the pool, Josh's friends rushed to his side.

"You didn't tell us that your dad was **a fart doctor!**" said Kenny excitedly.

The cat was out of the bag! Or should that be gas bag? thought Josh, sighing heavily.

"Yeah, he knows everything about farting! How random is that!" added Mitch.

"Look, he's not exactly called a fart doctor, he's a gastro ..."

"Well, that's what he told us!" said Pete, cutting Josh off.

"He did?"

"Yeah, cause Kenny couldn't say gastro ... um ... grastroenta ..."

"Gastroenterologist," said Josh.

"Yeah, so then your Dad said, 'If it's any easier, think of me as a fart doctor, but keep that to yourselves!'" added Pete.

A few moments later Mr Hewitt joined the boys, brushing water off his arms.

"Phew! That was great!" he announced.

"Um, Mr H, I have a question," coughed Pete. "Why do farts make a sound?"

"Hey, let's go down the Twist of Death slide," blurted Josh, trying desperately to change the subject.

But it was no use. His dad had his friends' full attention.

"Well, Pete, that's a good question," he began. "The **sound is created by the vibrations** around the opening of your bottom."

"*Dad!*" huffed Josh.

Mr Hewitt continued.

" . . . and the sound depends on the speed at which the gas is released."

"Cool!" echoed Josh's friends.

"So, which slide to next?" asked Mr Hewitt, clapping his hands together.

"I think you should skip this one, Dad," grumbled Josh. "Why don't you go and hang out with Mom!"

Josh turned to see his mother sitting under a shade of a tree, waving back at them.

"Well, if that's what you want," croaked Mr Hewitt.

"No! You hang out with us!" protested Josh's friends.

"Yeah, we want to ask you more questions!" they added.

"Well, the majority rules, son," shrugged Mr Hewitt as he and Josh's friends took off to the next slide.

Josh couldn't believe it. The very thing he hoped wouldn't happen today was happening right in front of him. His dad made it all about him—again. He had lost count of all the times his father would take over various situations with endless discussions about his job. From parent-teacher interviews to sitting next to total strangers on planes and trains, Josh's dad would always come around to **the topic of farting**. Josh used to think it was cool but now it was wearing very, very thin—especially when it was supposed to be *his* day.

But now he was in a jam. His friends liked his dad and if he said anything to stop his father from paying attention to them it would look bad

for him. He would come off looking like some miserable stick-in-the-mud. Josh had no choice but to grit his teeth and put up with it.

And put up with it he did. For the entire afternoon, in between all their slides, his friends bombarded his father with fart questions.

Why do farts stink? Do boys fart more than girls? Why do dog farts smell more than human farts? What's the difference between a fart and a burp? Is it unhealthy to hold in your farts?

Question after question after question, and Mr Hewitt was more than happy to answer every single one of them.

When it came to the end of the day and Josh's friends were dropped off at their homes, Josh was fuming.

"You have a great bunch of friends there!" declared Mr Hewitt, looking into the rear-view mirror at Josh.

Josh didn't answer his father. His lips were pursed and his arms were crossed.

"Did you hear me?"

Josh didn't budge.

"Looks like someone is upset with me. Am I right?"

"Of course he's upset with you," chimed in Mrs Hewitt. "You hijacked his day with your incessant talk about your job! Who wouldn't be upset?"

"Hang on!" said Mr Hewitt, raising his voice as he pulled into the driveway of their home. "Hijack is a little harsh, don't you think? Those boys enjoyed my company. They were having fun!"

"*They* may have been having fun," said Mrs Hewitt. "But your son wasn't."

"What are you talking about? He loved it! He had a ball! Didn't you, buddy?"

Mr Hewitt took off his seat belt and turned to face Josh. Josh raised his head and stared at his father. His heart was racing and felt as if his head was about to explode. He wanted to shout to his dad, I wish you weren't a gastroenterologist! I wish you didn't go on about it all the time! I wish you had just let my friends and me hang out, without trying to impress us. I wish you didn't always talk to complete strangers about something as dumb as farting. And I wish you hadn't totally **ruined my birthday**.

But he didn't have to. The look on his face had said it all to his dad.

Josh hopped out of the car and made his way to his bedroom.

Several minutes later, there was a knock at the door.

"Um, hey, you . . . " stuttered Josh's dad as he slowly stepped toward him. "I've just spoken to your mom and we've decided to skip dinner and have more of your birthday cake instead. Good idea, huh?"

Josh remained silent. Spread out on his bed with

his hands behind his head, he didn't take his eyes off the ceiling.

"Look," croaked Mr Hewitt, "I'm so sorry. I've really messed up big time, haven't I? I was selfish and inconsiderate. I just got carried away 'cause I love my job so much. But I know that shouldn't be an excuse. Your mother was right. She's always right. I'm sorry for hijacking your day and taking the attention away from you. Anyway, from now on I'm going to try **not to talk about flatus**, outside working hours, ever again. I promise. I hope you'll forgive me."

Josh didn't say a word. He heard his father sigh and turn to leave.

"Dad!" he called after him.

"I forgive you," he said.

His father smiled.

"And since you answered all my friends' questions today, *I* have a question for you," Josh added.

"Sure! Of course! Ask me anything you want," said Mr Hewitt excitedly.

"Do you think it was Mom that let one rip in the car earlier today?" Josh grinned at his dad.

"Most definitely!"

AND NOW, THE SEQUEL TO THE BEST-SMELLING FARTICUS MAXIMUS STORY YOU READ EARLIER IN THIS BOOK . . .

IX. FARTICUS
MAXIMUS II
The Fury of
Gassius
Brutus

CHAPTERUS ONE

THE RETURN OF ONE MEAN-LOOKING GLADIATOR

While the citizens of Toizarus, a village not far from Rome, were sound asleepus, a dark, giant figure on horseback rode silently into town.

"Did you hear that?" gasped twelve-year-old Billius Rex, sitting up in his bed.

"Hear what?" groaned his older brother, Kennius.

"That!" whispered Billius. "The sound of a horse clip-clopping past our window!"

"It's probably just a soldier," mumbled Kennius. "Go back to sleepus."

"It doesn't make sense! Soldiers travel in pairs or larger numbers, never by themselves," said Billius,

now getting out of bed and going over to the window. "And what's that rotten smell?"

"Probably the soldier's horse!"

As Kennius rolled over and shoved his head under his pillow, Billius carefully peeked out the window; he didn't want the stranger to see him.

Billius gasped again.

"I don't believe it!" he said, pulling his head back inside. "He's alive!"

Billius's heart was racing. He peeked again to make sure he wasn't dreaming. He wasn't. Under the moonlit sky, the figure having a drink from a fountain turned and glared in Billius's direction. Billius gulped and pulled back from the open window.

"Kennius, wake up!"

"What? What's going on?"

"I just saw **Black Dog Brutus!**"

"Now I know you're dreaming!" scoffed Kennius, sitting up. "Black Dog Brutus is dead!"

"Kennius, I'm not making this up!" huffed Billius. "Take a look for yourself if you don't believe me."

Kennius hopped out of bed, and when he made his way over to the window his eyes popped out of his head.

"You're right!" he croaked. "That is Black Dog Brutus!"

"Told you so!"

"Unless . . ."

"Unless what?" asked Billius.

"Unless it's not Black Dog but in fact his twin brother, Gassius!" said Kennius. "That would explain the **rotten smell** wafting this way."

"Twin brother!?" exclaimed Billius.

"Yes, twin brother. Everyone knows that Black Dog had an identical twin brother named Gassius. But when they were kids they lost their father in a horse and cart accident and their mother sent Gassius off to live with her cousins in Britannia."

Billus shook his head in disbelief. Kennius continued.

"She couldn't cope with raising two boys on her own. I think everyone in the village was happy with her decision, because as it turned out Gassius had **a gassius problem**. I think he was born Cassius, but that was soon changed to Gassius. He was a stinky little boy and, going by that smell, it doesn't seem as if things have changed much."

"HEY, YOU BOYS OVER THERE!" came a big booming voice.

"I SEE YOU SPYING ON ME! COME OUT HERE. I WANT TO ASK YOU SOMETHING!"

Billius's knees trembled as he looked to his brother to see what they should do. Gassius's unexpected loud and gruff voice scared the living poopus out of them. In fact, his shouting had woken up most of the village.

Kennius and Billius nervously made their way out to meet Gassius. Other villagers, including the mayor, also shuffled out into the street; like the Rex boys, many thought that Black Dog Brutus had returned from the dead. That was until Gassius spoke again.

"You boys and the good folk of this village. My name is **Gassius Brutus**. I've come a long way to see my mother and my brother. Can someone tell me where they are?"

Billius looked to his brother and his fellow villagers. No one was game to speak up.

"He's dead!" squeaked Billius.

"What are you doing?" choked Kennius.

"He needs to know!"

"HE'S WHAT?" growled Gassius.

Gassius marched over to Billius. He was a giant of a man. He had musclesusses on top of his musclesusses and his thighs were as thick as tree trunks. And the **smell shooting from his bottomus** was out of this world. Billius almost keeled over.

The mayor of the village quickly stepped in.

"Welcome back to Toizarus, Gassius!" he

stuttered nervously.

"I SAID, WHERE IS MY BROTHER, OLD MAN!"

"Your brother Black Dog was a great gladiator," said the mayor. "But unfortunately, he was butterfly-kissed a long time ago by a greater gladiator, Farticus Maximus. I'm terribly sorry."

Gassius snorted. He sneered. **He farted**. And snorted again, before saying, "And my mother?"

"Unfortunately," gulped the mayor, trying not to breathe in Gassius's silent but deadly wind, "she passed away shortly after Black Dog's death. It was too much for her. She died of a lonely heart. Again, I'm sorry Gassius. So, will you be staying . . . can we get you anything? Deodorant? Perfume? Draw you a nice hot bubble bath or perhaps a . . ."

"ENOUGH!" snapped Gassius. "I WILL FIGHT THIS FARTICUS MAXIMUS! MAN AGAINST MAN! GLADIATOR AGAINST GLADIATOR! FARTER AGAINST FARTER!"

"Um, so sorry again," coughed the mayor. "But Farticus retired, about a year ago. He went out on top—as **the greatest gladiator of all time**. He no longer fights!"

"WELL, HE WILL WHEN I FIND HIM! HE WILL BE FIGHTING FOR HIS LIFE! I AM BRITANNIA'S GREATEST GLADIATOR

AND I WILL AVENGE MY BROTHER
AND MOTHER'S DEATH. THIS FARTICUS
MAXIMUS WILL BE DEAD MEATUS WHEN I
FINISH WITH HIM!"

CHAPTERUS TWO

LOOK AT US NOW!

"Boys!" cried Rhina. "I've got some lovely pomegranate juice for you all. I think you should take a break!"

With ceramic cups in one hand and a jug in the other, Rhina trudged over to her beloved husband, Farticus Maximus, and poured him a drink.

"Happy anniversarus, my smellius one!" she smiled.

Farticus sipped his juice and kept a watchful eye on Rhina's father, Sinus Blockus, as he taught three young boys to wrestle goats.

"Anniversarus of what?" he asked.

"Today, exactly one year ago, you had your last gladiator battle," Rhina said glowingly. "And look at us now. **Look how far we've come!**"

Farticus glanced over Rhina's shoulder to see the life he had created since retiring as one of the greatest Roman gladiators of all time. She was

right; they had come a long way.

Farticus smiled proudly to see the luxurious ten-bedroomus villa next to the abandoned farmhouse he grew up in.

He also took pleasure in seeing his mother lead behind-the-farting-legend tour groups around his property and hold small how-to-make-orange-scented-snotus-rag workshops. In fact, she was currently in the middle of a tour. The tourists

waved at Farticus from across the field. Farticus
waved back and offered them a little something
they weren't expecting—a rip-roaring, rumbling,
deep-from-within-the-guts, humungous fart!

"YEAH! LONG LIVE FARTICUS!" the tourists
cheered and applauded.

Fortunately, they were some distance away and were standing upwind from Farticus.

"Oh, you showoff," grinned Rhina.

But there was one thing that Farticus was more proud of than anything else in his first year of retirement: the opening of an orphanage-slash-gladiator school (which was attached to his swanky villa) for kids that had been abandoned by their parents because of their **flatulence problems**, but who also harboured dreams of becoming mighty gladiators. He called it, *The Farticus Maximus Gladiator School and Orphanage for Kids that Stink*.

So far, the school had only three live-in smelly orphans-slash-gladiator students. And while numbers were expected to grow, Farticus looked upon these three orphan boys as if they were his own children.

There was Stinkius, Odorus, and Rotteneggus. All aged ten.

"Okay, boys," instructed Sinus. "Get ready to stun your goats . . . bottomusses in position . . . now, let 'em rip!"

Odorus stunned his goat with a silent but deadly stinker to the face—**PHOOOPH!!**—while Rotteneggus and Stinkius went for long, loud, classic wind-breakers that blew their goats off the ground—

BBBRRRRRRPPPPPPPP!!!!!!

"LONG LIVE FARTICUS!" the tourists cheered again.

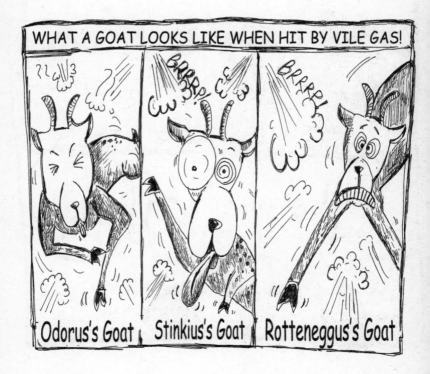

WHAT A GOAT LOOKS LIKE WHEN HIT BY VILE GAS!

Odorus's Goat   Stinkius's Goat   Rotteneggus's Goat

"Well, my boys," said Farticus, stepping in. "You've made great progress today and I think we should . . ."

Something caught Farticus's attention.

"What's wrong?" asked Sinus.

"I thought I saw something in the woods," croaked Farticus, as he **passed gas again**.

"LONG LIVE FARTICUS!" the tourists roared again.

"What was it?" asked Rhina.

"It looked like a giant man . . . staring at us?"

Everyone followed Farticus's gaze across the fields toward the nearby dark forest.

"Well, whatever it was, it's not there now," said Sinus. "Maybe you imagined it? Come on, boys! That's it for the day. Pick up your stunned goats and take them back to their pens."

"Yeah, maybe I did imagine it," mumbled Farticus, who knew deep down that he hadn't.

A dark, mysterious figure was watching him and he suspected it **wasn't a friendly fart-loving tourist**.

CHAPTERUS THREE

EVIL GASSIUS

"ARRRGHHHHH! FARTICUS!!!!"

Farticus jolted out of his sleep and sprang to his feet. Everyone was awakened by the spine-chilling scream at dawn.

"HELP! FARTICUS!" came the distressed voice.

It was Farticus's mother.

Farticus and the three smelly orphans rushed outside to see Farticus's mother in the clutches of a large musclesusses, evil-looking giant of a man.

"STAY WHERE YOU ARE OR THIS SNOTUS-RAG-WEARING LADY GETS IT!" he warned.

"Who are you! What do you want from us?" gulped Farticus, frightened for his mom.

"I am the great Gassius Brutus of Britannia, and I'm here to take the life of the man who took my brother's life!" growled the stranger. "Are you the great Farticus Maximus?"

"That is I!" said Farticus, stepping forward.

"I SAID DON'T MOVE OR ELSE . . ."

Farticus froze.

"Huh! You don't look like the greatest gladiator of all time," mumbled Gassius, as he strengthened his grip around Farticus's mother's neck. "You look rather **puny and pathetic!**"

"Blow him away, Master!" whispered Odorus.

"Yeah, let him have it!" added Rotteneggus.

"Yeah, let one rip!" said Stinkius.

"I challenge you to a battle to the death. You butterfly-kissed my brother, Black Dog, now it's your turn to suffer!"

"**Blow him away**, son!" croaked Farticus's mother. "Don't worry about hurting me, I'm wearing my super-dooper five-layered orange-scented snotus rag. Just hurry up and blow this biggus doofus away!"

Gassius ripped off the snotus rag from Farticus's mother's face.

"Ooops!" cried Farticus mother. "I should've kept my big mouth shut!"

"Let my mother go!" ordered Farticus. "If you are a real gladiator then you have no business with a poor, defenceless old woman. Release her and be a man. Take me on!"

"I thought you no longer fight," sneered Gassius,

pushing Farticus's mother aside.

"I don't!" began Farticus. "Not since my wife and manager suggested . . ."

It suddenly dawned on Farticus that Rhina and Sinus were nowhere to be seen. Why had they stayed inside all this time? *How strange*, thought Farticus.

"FARTICUS, LOOK OUT!" shouted Rotteneggus. "He's about to let one rip!"

Before Farticus knew what was happening, Gassius blustered him off his feet with a colossal, **triple-whammy bottumus explosion**. Farticus hit the ground hard, stunned by the velocity and vileness of Gassius's gas.

Never in Farticus's life had he encountered someone who had the same flatulence power he did.

"And that's why they call me the Great Gassius!" Gassius cackled loudly. **"Now to finish you off!"**

CHAPTERUS FOUR

RHINA?

Gassius pulled out his sword and rushed for Farticus. Farticus rose to his feet, still wobbly and stunned. He coughed and spluttered as Gassius's stink cloud lingered like a bad . . . well, like a bad smell.

"We'll help you, Farticus!" yelled Odorus.

Odorus, Stinkius and Rotteneggus charged at Gassius.

"NO!" yelled Farticus.

"Oh, my goodness!" screamed Farticus's mom, watching all this from afar.

But it was too late.

Gassius whipped around and blasted the three orphan boys with wind that would make a three-thousand-tonne elephant fall to its knees.

Farticus rushed to the stunned boys' side. As he tried to revive them he was unaware that the evil Gassius was looming behind with his **sword raised** above his head, ready to butterfly-kiss him with a single blow.

"NOOOOO!!!!!" screamed Rhina, rushing out of the villa. "GASSY, DON'T!"

"Rhina?" stuttered Gassius. "Rhina Blockus, is that you?"

"Gassy?" croaked Farticus.

CHAPTERUS FIVE

WHAT THE . . .

By the time the orphan boys had come to, Farticus had learned that Rhina, his beloved wife, and Gassius, the evil-smelling giant of a gladiator from Britannia who was only seconds away from ending his life, actually *knew* each other.

Farticus was dumbfounded.

"Now, let me get this straightus," he said, turning to Rhina and Sinus. "You both lived in Britannia before you met me?"

Rhina and Sinus nodded.

"And you knew *him*!" Farticus added, pointing to Gassius.

"She not only knew me, loser," exclaimed Gassius. "I was her boyfriend. We were **engaged to get married!**"

"What the . . . ?" gasped Farticus, who found this

shocking news to be far more painful than any
gladiator battle he had ever been in.

"Yeah," continued Gassius. "But she left me.
Vanished. I looked everywhere for her. She broke
my heart."

"I thought you were dead!" blurted Rhina. "Daddy
and I were told by one of your generals that you
were butterfly-kissed at the Battle of Mushypeas.

My heart was broken. Daddy suggested that we should move to Rome and make a fresh start. So, we did. And then I met Farticus."

Farticus was stunned. He didn't know what to say. Gassius was also speechless. Actually, it was an awkward moment for everyone. The silence was deafening . . . that is, until Farticus dropped another stink bomb.

"LONG LIVE FARTICUS!"

"Oh, my! That's my first tour group of the day," exclaimed Farticus's mother, seeing a group of tourists appear over the horizon. "Sorry, I can't stay, must dash!"

Farticus's mother rushed off to greet her tour group.

"Well, now that you know I'm alive, we can be together again," croaked Gassius.

"You what?" snapped Farticus.

"Gassy . . ." said Rhina softly. "I'm with Farticus now. I'm sorry."

"Yeah, and don't you forget it, you uglyus muggus," added Farticus.

Gassius's nostrilusses began to flare. His eyes darkened and he snarled like a hungry wolf.

"Then I have another reason to pulverize you," he growled.

"Look out. **He's about to blow again!**" yelled Odorus.

"Run, boys!" shouted Sinus.

The three orphans sprinted back toward the villa.

But this time Farticus was ready. He got into battle position: he swung around and pointed his bottomus toward the great Gassius.

"Bring it on!" he said under his breath.

CHAPTERUS SiX

IN THE NAME
OF THE EMPEROR!

"Farticus! Gassius! Don't fight over me," pleaded
Rhina.

"You're worth fighting for," replied Gassius and
Farticus in unison.

This infuriated the stinky gladiators even more. "WAIT!" hollered Sinus. "LOOK!"

Everyone turned to see a troop of Roman soldiers marching over the horizon. As they drew nearer, Farticus could see that they were all, including their horses, wearing orange-scented snotus rags.

"In the name of the Emperor, I order you to **put down your deadly bottomusses!**"

cried the leader of the troop, General Secondus Fiddlus. "And to not let one rip while we're in your presence."

Farticus and Gassius reluctantly lowered their bottomusses as the general went on to say, "The Emperor has found out that you two are about to battle . . ."

"How do you know that already?" asked Farticus.

"That's not important!" snapped General Fiddlus. "Let's just say we have eyes and ears everywhere and that biggus brotherus is watching you. Anyway, the Emperor wants you two to battle it out at the Colosseum. Spectator numbers are down since you left, Farticus, and your battle with Gassius will be a humungous boost to the sport."

"But I've retired," said Farticus.

"Well, as of now you are **out of retirement**. You are scheduled to battle seven days from now at the Colosseum. If you don't show up we are ordered to take your life. If you refuse me now, we are ordered to **take your life immediately**. So, really, you have no choice. And this goes for you, too, Gassius of Britannia. And by the way, we've already had the posters printed up."

The general rolled out a poster.

It read: *Get Out Your Snotus Rags for the Greatest Stink-Off Battle of the Century at the Coloseum next Satadaius. The Legendary Farticus Maximus Versus the Great Gassius Brutus of Britannia. HURRY! Tickets Sold at Your Localus Outlets.*

"I can't believe this is happening," Rhina began to sob. "Please, General, tell me that this won't be a **battle to the death!**"

"Huh! You've got to be kidding, woman!" scoffed the general. "This is ancient Rome. We love to see blood. And if we're lucky, these two putrid-smelling gladiators will butterfly-kiss *each other* in the process. It will be a double-whammy!"

Rhina burst into tears, dropping her head onto

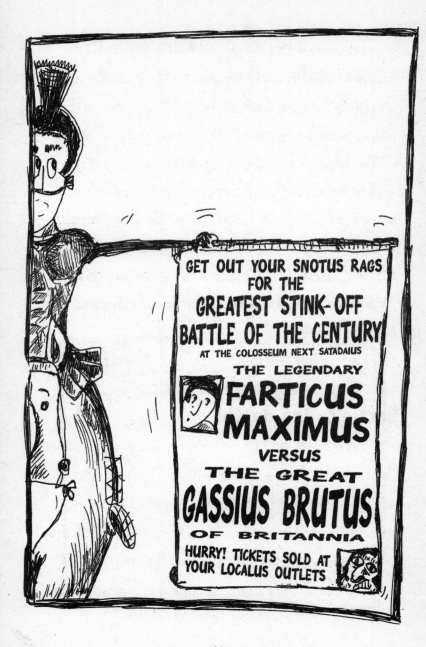

Farticus's shoulder.

Gassius glared at Farticus.

Farticus glared back at him.

Sinus looked worried.

The general and the soldiers chuckled loudly before riding off into the distance. Gassius glared again . . . and Farticus, well, he **nervously broke wind**.

"LONG LIVE FARTICUS!" cheered the tourists.

Farticus gulped. That's what he was hoping!

WILL FARTICUS SURVIVE THE
GREATEST BATTLE OF HIS LIFE?
OR DOES THIS SPELL ... OR SHOULD WE SAY,
SMELL, THE END FOR OUR WINDY HERO?

WILL RHINA EVER STOP CRYING EVEN THOUGH
SHE SECRETLY LOVES IT THAT TWO STINKY
GLADIATORS WILL BE FIGHTING
TO WIN HER HEART?

WILL FARTICUS'S MOTHER BECOME
THE RICHEST WOMAN IN THE ROMAN EMPIRE WITH
HER ENTERPRISING BUSINESSES?

WILL THE THREE ORPHANS GROW UP TO FOLLOW
FARTICUS'S FARTSTEPS?

FIND OUT IN THE NEXT
RIP-ROARING ADVENTURE ...

FARTICUS MAXIMUS iii
THE STINK-OFF BATTLE OF THE CENTURY

(and MORE stories that reek!)

COMING VERY SOON!